The Tree Neil Ward

Raindrop Press

First Published in Great Britain in 2020 by
Raindrop Press Ltd
www.raindroppress.co.uk

ISBN 978-0-9957221-0-1

Printed by BookPrintingUK
www.bookprintinguk.com

Distributed in Great Britain by
Raindrop Press Ltd

For My Beautiful Mum

Acknowledgements

This book began as a personal diary, written in order to help me cope with living in this world.

The practice of writing enabled me to reflect and meditate upon my experiences each day and this in turn directly led to sensations of peace and calm. Inspired by these feelings, my diary became a journal of drawings and recurring insights.

Slowly, as sensitivity and love towards myself grew, the characters of Alice and Bertie emerged. I worked to find a way to express my emotions more deeply and the simple pencil drawings developed into detailed colourful illustrations, that I began to share with others.

Although daunted by the idea of writing a book, responses to the illustrations encouraged me to create a simple and expressive form of words that further revealed aspects of the world as it appears to me.

Many people have influenced my thinking during the development of this book:

Alice, getting to know you, as you sold ice creams on the river boat in York, inspired the characters of Alice and Bertie.

Susan, the difficult circumstances of your life gave rise to anger, fear, hope and compassion - compelling me to seek a path of tolerance and understanding both for myself and others. These insights have ultimately found expression in this book.

Lily, I saw within you a caring person who, like many of us, was struggling to find her place in this world. Your striving prompted me to write about the precious nature of who we can be.

Keith, your social conscience calmed me and kept alive the truth that we are more important to one another than we might first recognise. This understanding has influenced a great deal of what I have written about.

Ceri, without our friendship, I would not have got this far. The kindness and care that we have shared for one another, and your enthusiasm towards Alice and Bertie, helped me greatly to continue.

Harry, our 'chance' encounters and our passionate, uplifting conversations encouraged me to write with conviction of the invaluable opportunities that exist for each of us every day.

Vajraloka, my heartfelt appreciation for the inspiring example of compassion, tolerance and care that is offered by the community. You have enabled me to rest more deeply with my experiences. Your influence over the years is reflected throughout this book.

Edward, my visits to The Tree, and our thoughtful discussions, changed the course of this work. Your interest and enthusiasm helped greatly to shape and develop my ideas.

Claire, it has been a pleasure to portray in this story the kindness that you have always shown towards me at The Tree.

Julie, our discovery of a shared connection hinted at the mystery of life that I have sought to echo within this story.

Maggie, the commitment and enthusiasm you put into creating something special at Dale Head Farm Tea Garden inspired me to continue to do the same with my creative endeavours. Your opinion on an early draft helped give me the reassurance that I needed to develop the writing in its current form.

Julia, Steve and the staff at the Pig & Pastry, your kindness and interest, combined with your delicious hot soups, helped me to feel safe and nurtured when I walked in feeling hungry, tired and isolated after a morning of creative toil.

Jessie, you allowed me to be heard when others were unable to. When I came to write this book, remembering our conversations helped me so much to trust in my view of the world.

Jacquie, your willingness to travel this path with me, and the strong, loving connection that we share, has resulted in you being a resilient creative force with whom I can discuss, argue and deliberate. Your open-hearted generosity, as well as your skilful and sensitive approach to editing, has enabled me to portray as clearly as possible the reality that I see.

Mum, you showed me that it is possible to live, thrive and succeed with love, honesty and compassion. Your unwavering support and interest in my artistic ability has been a constant source of strength that has helped me to pursue a gentle path of creativity. Knowing that you love me and embrace my emotional sensitivities sustained me through the lengthy task of writing this book.

Contents

Illustrations

Introduction

How incredibly fortunate I am to feel pain and suffering so deeply. My sensitivities give me little real choice but to change and grow.

On a good day, this is exactly how I view my life. The things that irritate, upset and annoy me are sources of pain from which I can alter my view of the world and my importance in it.

This outlook has been arrived at through a long process of trial and error.

Trying to fight the world, I have found, does not work. It is bigger than I am. It can - and does - crush me every time. Attempting to impose my views upon the world does not work either. So often I have rallied against the realities of this world... only to lose.

What a magnificent, precious gift! I cannot get my own way. Instead, I have to learn that life is in control - not me.

And what are the realities in this world?

I experience everything as being in a constant state of change - nothing is ever still. Events, people, circumstances and situations that I am familiar with and attached to change or cease to exist.

I don't like this reality - and yet I cannot escape it. I am so completely entwined and enmeshed within this uncertain, unstable existence and yet I crave security and stability.

So, what can I do?

I can kick, scream, complain, get angry and feel bitterness; all of which I have done plenty of - and will doubtless lapse back into doing again. Or, as I discovered by accident and in desperation, I can find ways of quietly and gently understanding the din and racket going on inside me.

In the beginning this felt like an almost impossible task - and I didn't really know what I was doing. Describing this inward journey of thoughts, feelings and emotions is what I have attempted to do in this book.

Alice and Bertie have guided, comforted, inspired and helped me to overcome fear and anger; to be strong and to feel love, compassion and patience towards myself as well as others. They remind me that we are all doing the best that we can.

They seem to arise from a beautiful place that lies beyond the upset, panic, worry and controlling confusion of my weary and often chaotic mind.

They seem to exist in a part of my being that terrifies, yet also inspires me because it lies beyond words and understanding.

It is a place of mystery. A place that seems much older than me. A place of wisdom that appears to 'know' why I am here, what my purpose is and who I am. It is certainly a realm of stillness and quiet - and is undoubtedly where I experience peace.

Although it takes some effort to find and experience this aspect of myself, I keep doing so because it is the best way I have found of accepting with greater ease the realities of life.

Occasionally, I am even moved to tears as I catch a glimpse of the precious nature of my being human.

I hope very much that in creating this work and sharing my story with you, through Alice and Bertie, it will encourage and inspire you to discover this same amazing realm within yourself; a place that the mind cannot enter, yet the heart knows well.

Prologue

Gazing through swirls of steam rising slowly from her tea, Alice peers out of the window onto the busy street below.

Golden morning sunlight illuminating rooftops, ivy shimmering on a wall and an expanse of clear blue sky stir a primitive part of her that lies beyond words.

Another car edges into the small street where she lives; the driver looking for a space to park in this ever-moving city.

"Am I just running away... or should I really take this break?" thinks Alice.

Resting her head in her hands, she murmurs, "I am so worn out with trying to make sense of it all."

Half-closed curtains cast sharp, deep shadows around the room that echo a downhearted place within her. Tired and exhausted, she sinks into the sofa, "I do need to rest!" she exclaims. Bertie, lifting his head from under his soft, wispy tail, glances wide-eyed towards her.

Staring hopefully at the leaflet in her hand, "Can I do this?" she sighs, reflecting upon how beautiful The Tree looks, nestled peacefully amongst rolling hills.

For weeks now, she has been looking forward to this trip; an opportunity to rest, relax and be taken care of. Yet, in spite of her excitement and relief, the anticipation of having space and time alone feels almost overwhelming.

On this, the morning of her departure, Alice feels tense as she struggles to let go. "What am I doing?" she questions under her breath, concerned that she might not be able to cope with the bubbling emotions already surfacing.

Although sitting in the safe familiarity of this room, she is burdened by an uneasiness that will not shift.

"I have to try something new," she reminds herself earnestly.

The leaflet, still held gently, offers her comfort once more. "The food looks delicious," she anticipates excitedly, feeling almost elated at the prospect of not having to cook for herself.

The pull of the cloudless blue sky and sound of birdsong outside feels ever more intense, and she senses a relaxed freedom and hope for the mystery unfolding within her.

The effort of not surrendering more deeply to these strong emotions - that have kept nagging at her for so long - has been exhausting. She realises that holding on is now only causing more pain.

Her face warmed by sunlight streaming through the window, she pauses and with growing confidence lifts her head. "Thank goodness I am giving myself a break. Perhaps having space and time to slow down and rest is all I really need?"

Contrasting sharply with the seemingly never-ending noise and busyness of her daily life, these words hurt.

Standing, she catches sight of herself in the mirror; beyond the tired and strained figure, she glimpses an inner world that flickers with energy and knowing.

Smiling at her reflection, Alice utters, "I do deserve this treat. I am allowed to be kind and caring towards myself," before turning and striding purposefully towards the door.

With Bertie scampering loyally behind her, she courageously declares, "I can take myself to a better place."

Arriving

Unsettled, Alice pulls herself along, untangling from her life. "I have so many things to do - so many problems to solve," she mutters.

"What good will this do?" Her mind is a crowd of worries as she treads wearily down the quiet, dimly-lit road.

"Bertie," she calls, "where are you?" Ears flopping, he turns his head, and quickly is by her side.

Tears fill her swollen eyes, "I am so tired and exhausted... I do need a break."

Distant purple-red light stretches like a ribbon of silk across this fading blue-grey sky. Awakening to this flash of beauty, a wave of nervous anticipation ripples through her.

Standing still, doubt momentarily evaporates.

"This is gorgeous!" she sighs, "What a breathtaking place!"

Surrounded by a stunning landscape of peaceful, unstirring hills that rise steadily on either side, she feels nestled and safe in this place of tranquillity.

Guilt, intense and piercing, grips her, "It is so beautiful and peaceful here - I don't know that I deserve this?"

Gazing ahead, her heart now racing, "I wonder if this is where I am meant to be?" she quietly reflects, turning to an untroubled Bertie.

A question grows louder in her mind, "Have I made the right choice?"

Nearing a window, Alice peers in to see a warm, cosy room and begins to feel a sense of relief. "I wonder what I will find here?" she ponders, steadily moving towards a welcoming light glowing gently through a glazed wooden door.

Feeling Safe

Pushing firmly on the white painted door, "This is our room," says Alice in excited anticipation to Bertie as she steps nervously inside. Wide-eyed, she smiles at the delightful, calming sight before her.

"Goodness - what a gorgeous room!" she gasps, as an eager Bertie dashes around.

Cosy pastel shades of blue and pink, a glow of gentle, comforting yellow light; this still and peaceful room is snug and calm.

"I can relax here," murmurs Alice knowingly.

The busy, persistent thoughts of her mind, that have caused her to feel so strained, begin to slow down. Recognising a place of safety, she rests her luggage on the floor.

"This feels like home," a sense of relief rises steadily in her voice. "The people here obviously care."

Long-forgotten childhood memories of feeling loved and protected echo within. Gazing through the tall sash window, her heart feels pulled deeper into the still, tranquil landscape beyond.

A tear trickles down her face. "I am so glad that I have decided to take care of myself for a while," this thought settling gently in her mind.

"I feel that I am safe and can rest, supported by these kind people."

Exhausted, Alice draws herself from the window.

Within a moment, she feels overwhelmed by a sense of weariness that tugs so deeply from within that she stands by the bed, allows herself to fall backwards and within a matter of seconds is fast asleep.

A Battle Within

Shivering, Alice and Bertie step into the cold damp of this overcast day and begin walking along an empty road that leads into the haze of the mist-covered dale.

Buried deep within this landscape, the usually green rolling hills are dull and grey-looking.

A nervous panic rising, she grips tightly onto her umbrella, "I am finding it harder to see," she frets anxiously.

Gazing upwards, thunderous, brooding clouds, heavy and black, are now directly overhead. Alice tenses as her face and hands sting in the sharp, fierce wind and icy-cold rain.

Struggling with a tangle of emotions, her umbrella blown inside out, she grips tightly, fearful of losing control.

"This is not what I came here for!" she howls, turning to a wet and dishevelled Bertie.

Her eyes tired, Alice battles on through the treacherous conditions, searching for a place to rest.

"This is much harder than I thought," she complains as a dull heaviness hauls and tugs from deep within.

Treading along this perilous path, with its terrifying howling wind, she feels fearful and alone yet, seeing a distant glimmer of light in the sky, remembers those who love her.

Struggling to hold these warm feelings with kindness, tension echoes in her voice, "I hope that I will be safe?", as she courageously continues to face this hostile place.

Bertie blown from side to side, the wind almost knocking Alice off her feet, the uncontrollable forces of this place wrench difficult emotions from within.

"I never wanted to feel like this!" she sobs.

A troubled frown burrows across her face, "This is all too much!"; her cries lost in the fierce din of the storm.

Ignited by the beautiful light in the sky, memories of being loved give rise to an unexpected glimpse of a faint, flickering inner beauty and strength.

Alice feels compelled to carry on, "I will trust and try to have faith," she resolves, turning into the storm.

4

Falling

Cold and tired, Alice and Bertie walk steadily on, pushing against the perishing, icy wind and piercing rain of this inhospitable place.

Feeling pride in her strength to continue, "I will trust in myself," she repeats, as if humming a long-forgotten song in her head.

Relief rises as, shadowy-grey through the damp, hazy mist, a trail leading to a sheltered spot appears.

Alice turns to Bertie, his long, thick hair soaked through. "We can rest over there for a while," she says hopefully. "Perhaps I have nothing to worry about after all?"

Away from the safety of the path, heading down this trail towards the protection of a large tree, her foot slips and instantly the muddy ground is gone.

Fear erupts in every fibre of her body; frantically panicking, she stretches out her arms grasping for something to hold... but there is nothing there.

Terrified, "No!" she screams in dread, as her body begins to fall helplessly. Braced for a painful landing, her muscles tense.

Fear unravels slowly in her mind as if time itself has slowed down and is now moving at a crawl.

Conceding that she has no control, "What can I rely on?" echoes a cry from within.

Tumbling backwards, in a moment that has no meaning at all, this precious woman, now vulnerable, feels frightened and alone.

With no choice but to accept the present conditions, the fear of falling loosens its grip.

"I have to trust!" she realises.

5

Fallen

Wind and driving rain besieging them, drenched, Alice hits the ground with a bump. "Ouch!" she wails, as a sharp pain shoots through her.

Suffering only a bruise, relief briefly turns to dismay. "My beautiful jacket!" she sobs, feeling torn fabric beneath her fingers.

Brooding emotions swell like an ocean crashing harshly against the golden, delicate sands of her mind.

Her face sheltered by her hands, "I thought I would be safe, following my heart," she mutters unhappily, drops of rain suspended from her lips.

"I feel so stupid," she mumbles, self-blame filling her voice.

"Why is life so difficult?" she screams, suddenly swept by a tide of emotion.

Exasperated and tired, her pain-choked voice falters in the air, "I haven't deserved this!"

Tugging lovingly at her shoelace, Bertie pushes misery to one side, transforming pity into strength in this grey, faded world that now surrounds her.

Alice turns to Bertie and forces a smile. "I must care about myself, just as you are caring for me," she sighs, before pulling

herself to her feet once more.

"What else can I do?" she reflects, a trembling self-care rising steadily in her voice as she finds her footing in the slippery, wet mud.

6

Seeing Connections

Bruised and shaken, Alice and Bertie proceed gingerly down the small, muddy track, eventually joining a quiet, narrow road that snakes and winds its way along the flat-lying ground, with the dale rising on either side.

Feeling confused, "What am I doing here?" she sniffles, peering down this wet, uneven road, lined on one side by an old stone wall, and on the other by a hawthorn hedge.

Stopping by a wooden gate, Alice glances over the wall and gazes upon a cheerless, soggy field, cold, wet sheep and a scrawny tree.

An ordinary sight: "There is nothing here," barks her mind, impatient to hurry her along.

Shivering, she continues to stand, intrigued by unfamiliar feelings rising from within.

"There is something here - but I am not yet sure what it is."

Out of the dullness of this dreary day begin to emerge inspiring, flowing trails of colourful light. Her breath slowing, "Look at this!" she gasps with astonishment and awe.

Growing in these difficult conditions, the spindly tree suddenly seems courageous and strong. "It is so beautiful," she says, captivated, "living in its own special way."

A fragile lamb is loved and warm, kept safe by its tired yet protective mother.

Witnessing these contradictions of life, a tear rolls down her face. Feeling humbled, she cries, "We all struggle!"

Loneliness falls away, as she realises with courage, "My pain is no different from that of anybody else."

A calm stillness settles within her. "I cannot avoid suffering, but I can grow - trusting in life to reveal more of what I hold inside."

7

Remembering

Alice and Bertie step inquisitively along a small gravel path that quickly leads to stepping stones meandering their way across the grass.

Delight shining in her eyes, she spots a swing dangling from a broad tree, its branches stretching high into the alluring, ocean-blue sky.

"I can't wait to have a go!" squeals Alice in anticipation.

Turning to a less-than-confident and slightly bemused-looking Bertie, "I haven't been on a swing for years," she reflects.

Joy momentarily gives way to sadness as memories from childhood erupt. A difficult path to follow, she continues walking towards the swing across the garden filled with fragments of light.

With Bertie holding on, childlike, and reminders of her life flickering through her mind, Alice grasps the thick, twisted rope firmly and pushes herself into the air.

A comforting, warm breeze blowing through her hair, these immediate sensations of freedom clash with a myriad of memories and recollections.

Afraid to feel this growing, complex fabric of life more deeply, Alice continues to push higher, her feet almost touching the leaves hanging from the tree. "I dare not stop," she thinks, as more afraid than ever that he might fall, Bertie grips even tighter.

Curiosity animates a cat, as creatures full of life expressing itself are attracted and intrigued by this unfolding moment.

Thoughts that give rise to feelings gradually emerge as emotions that bubble up... and a tear trickles down her face. As if an orchestral melody of life is playing from within her, Alice now glimpses a gateway to a mystifying truth, and is overwhelmed.

Dizzy and tired, "I had better stop and rest," she whispers, pushing no more. As she slows down, the swing gently comes to a halt.

8

Feeling Tired

Jewels of sparkling light flicker and dance across the wall and spines of the books in this charming, quiet, cosy room.

Small wooden boxes on the shelf above the fireplace spell out the word 'RELAX'.

With her legs tucked tightly into her body, Alice sits upright and begins to sink into the soft cushion of the spacious brown sofa that lies under the tall window.

Bertie, his nose glistening, is already resting beside her.

Tears appear in her tender, tired eyes as childhood memories continue to surface more intensely than ever.

Feeling confused, she looks all around, but realises that her family is not here to guide her. "I am alone," she whispers to herself.

Small muscles ache and her shoulders are tense, as her body and mind struggle against each other.

"How do I relax?" she asks, her sweet, soft voice full of questioning. "How do I rest?"

"It is as if my mind refuses to let go."

9

Struggling to Rest

Her mind a scattered web of thoughts frantically spinning and twisting out of control, this tranquil room closes in.

Rows of books sit cold and senseless on the shelves behind her; reminding Alice of a larger, more colourful world. Bertie, caring and concerned, lies quiet and still beside her.

Passions and thoughts surging, her body begins to tighten and tense as muscles pull and strain in every direction. Frothing and fizzing, instant by instant, the swelling discord of noise soon becomes deafening.

A spark of thought flits through the chaos of her mind. "Am I losing control?" she cries in muffled tones, just loud enough to break the silence of this room - but not too loud to draw attention to this private moment.

"Stop, stop!" she screeches angrily. Frustration seethes in her voice, "This is not what I came here for - I came here to relax!"

Moments later, a bubble of emotional energy bursts, giving way to an unexpected sense of stillness.

"What will happen if I just sit still?" her voice hushes.

A quiet, fragile thought forms. "What will happen if I no longer try to hide?"

10

Letting Go

Sitting criss-crossed and feeling knotted inside, thoughts whizz frantically around her head.

Alone, Alice feels pulled deeper and deeper into herself - towards a place she does not wish to go.

Overcome with tiredness, panic rises in her mind. "What am I going to do?" she murmurs.

"Is everything alright?" comes a voice filled with kindness from the direction of the door.

Her eyes springing open with a jolt, a stunned Alice replies, "I'm fine, thank you. Thank you," unable to reveal the world of emotions she feels inside.

"Good," comes the reply full of care, instantly cutting through the thoughts of her troubled mind like sunshine finding its way to the cold, forgotten leaves of a forest floor.

The panic of her mind now clear to see, her thoughts turn to the deep, loving gaze of her mother. "I am loved. I am so loved," she whispers in a calm, knowing voice.

"This world is so difficult," she acknowledges. The muscles of her body now relax, and her mind is able to let go.

No longer struggling, Alice soon falls fast asleep. Beside her, a reassured Bertie rests even more deeply than before.

11

A Wonderful Place

Alice lies peacefully, cocooned in a boundless world of colour, sound and light that gently shimmers and vibrates in all directions; as if an endless, rippling wave were flowing effortlessly to and fro.

Resting in this place that has no name, her mind perfectly calm and still, she observes a soft, tingling dance and play of every tiny sensation in her body.

Within a few moments, an uncontrolled fear disturbs this peace.

"I cannot move!" she cries.

Panicking, her body jolts back into the familiar objects of this room and, moment by moment, she watches with dismay as her mind once again begins to crowd with thoughts and ideas.

"What have I just experienced?" she wonders, excited yet unsure.

Her bare toes push gently outwards. "Bertie!" she exclaims, her mind now forced back into this room.

She pauses, considering carefully, "I can't remember having felt anything like this before."

Even now, looking around, colours are more intense, the flickering light around her almost alive. "This room has not changed," she realises warily, "Something is changing in me."

"Perhaps slowing down here has allowed me to touch upon something extraordinary... in the midst of ordinary life."

Beyond the cynicism of her doubting mind, she chooses to trust in this glimpse of life too deep to be held or described by words alone.

Looking across at Bertie, Alice smiles hesitantly. "I'm not sure where this will lead... but I will do my best to remain open to these feelings that offer me a new and different view of the world."

Unsettled yet energised by the possibilities ahead, Alice lifts herself to her feet, beckoning, "Come on Bertie... let's go for a walk."

12

The Dark Night

Stepping into the night, Alice gazes upon ribbons of fading purple-blue light that linger above dark, distant hills.

The cool night air echoes to the sound of an owl as they walk steadily along the quiet, dimly-lit road, eventually reaching a crossroads, to one side of which lies a small track.

Feeling compelled to carry on, she decides to walk with Bertie along this narrow, dark track.

Fear and uncertainty grow. "What am I doing here?" she falters, self-doubt rising within her voice as if the ground under her feet has turned to mud.

"I feel scared, Bertie - maybe we should return home and leave The Tree altogether?"

Like a mountain rising within her, this place feels far too difficult to navigate alone, yet Alice continues to put one foot in front of another.

"Is there something here for me to discover?" she whispers, her words evaporating into the cool night air.

Seconds later, out of the shadowy darkness, appears a large wooden gate that is half-open.

13

A Precious Sight

Unaffected by feeling cold and tired, Alice and Bertie walk cautiously through the gate into the darkness, intrigued by a faint, distant light.

Surrounded by shadows, Alice catches sight of higgledy-piggledy planks of wood, a lopsided roof and a wonky door ajar spilling a soft yellow glow into the inky black night.

"Goodness!" she gasps to Bertie, "A cockerel shed!"

All is still. A flash of brilliance. Hair flopping, she lifts her head skyward and falls into a thousand, million stars.

Soft lips trembling, "I feel so small," she sighs.

Spellbound, Alice returns her gaze to the rickety wooden shack - imperfect, tumble-down - but a safe, warm home for a small creature on this earth.

Tears stream down her face, her arm shakes as she steadies herself in the darkness.

"I... I am only a small creature too!"

Sadness rising within her, she asks, "Do I have a light within me?"

14

Flickering Shadows

Glimmers of light flicker in the darkness, illuminating a loneliness and despair that Alice now feels.

Logs blaze with intense yellow-red flames that burn brightly, before fading into smouldering embers. Holding Bertie tightly, "How can I sustain a belief in myself?' she whispers. "How can I remember, in each moment, that I am beautiful?"

Long dark shadows speak to her doubt and vulnerability. Contemplating this hectic world, she questions, "How can I possibly believe that there is a place for the light within me?"

Bertie turns his head, his dark brown eyes full of love. Her heart momentarily lifts from this place of many shadows.

"I want to experience the freedom that following an inner truth might bring... yet I am afraid of discovering it is nothing more than a hopeful dream in a random, chaotic world."

Immersed in this moment, Alice becomes aware of light fading to darkness, and gloominess transforming into light.

"The shadows that I carry inside are only as real as I allow them to be. If instead I follow the fragments of light within, these will guide me to discover the truth of who I am."

Seeing a way forward in this life of many lights, "Alice," she acknowledges bravely, "You must create this path for yourself."

15

Early Morning

Wrapped up safe and warm, Alice lies fast asleep in this dimly-lit room. With Bertie downstairs, she is lost amid vivid dreams.

From beyond the curtain-covered window of this cosy room, a distant cockerel crows, nearby lambs and sheep bleat, a wood-pigeon coos mellow sounds and small birds chirp and sing to one another.

Startled, she opens her eyes into a room full of shadows before mumbling, "What are these sounds?"

Dreams continue to drift in and out of her mind, her resting body is filled with emotion and then, a moment of stillness.

Footsteps gently patter across the roof.

"A dawn chorus!" she giggles.

"I don't feel scared, something has changed."

Reminded of the hills and beautiful walk, of lambs sheltered safe and warm next to their mothers, her heart is soothed and glad to be here as she gently allows her mind time to adjust.

Breakfast

Her face beaming as he bounds towards her, Alice cuddles Bertie before sitting at the large wooden table that fills this calm room and looks out across the rolling hills of this spectacular dale.

Appearing before her, a masterpiece of sunny yellow scrambled eggs, bright red grilled tomatoes, hearty beans, delicious-looking fried mushrooms and four thick slices of hot toast.

A tear gently trickles down her face, as she thinks to herself, "I feel so taken care of and loved."

With Bertie close by and content with a bowl of food, warm, inviting memories of being close to her family emerge, and tingle throughout her body.

Still puzzled by the changes that she is experiencing at The Tree, a reflection in the coffee pot catches her eye.

"Oh gosh," she quietly murmurs, "this reflection is like my mind - constantly moving and changing - distorting the world around me."

"Yet my heart seems to know what is right," she thinks, before eagerly tucking into her food.

"How, then," Alice wonders, "do I trust in my heart?"

Sitting Quietly

Electric blue sky and peach-red sun gently kiss the landscape as Alice and Bertie walk along this quiet, river-like road that flows through steeply rising hills.

The question returns. "How do I trust in my heart?"

A short while later, a small wooden bench invites Alice to sit.

Fidgeting, she asks Bertie, "What am I going to do?" before memories of resting in the lounge, and the peaceful place she found there, return.

"I will just sit," a calmness growing steadily in her voice.

Coffee pot reflections move to and fro. Watching her restless mind, she sits serene, remembering the mystery that lies beyond this noisy, clackety din of thoughts.

Beauty radiating, her mind quietening, hushed, she feels birds sing with each of her senses tingling. While leaves gently rustle, a cool breeze washes harmoniously around this courageous woman with strength enough to believe in herself.

"All things must change, and I have nothing to fear," she calmly whispers.

"My heart already knows why I am here."

18

A Hidden Path

R ising to her feet, Alice gently smiles, "Let's discover where to go."

Gazing steadily and still at the nearby noticeboard, three small signs catch her eye:

'The History Society presents Dr. Alice Green - dates to follow'
'Your mysterious tour of West Dalton Wood, by J. B. Nightly'
'Eat well for a healthy heart - your local health clinic'

Awakening in this moment, she sees within these words: 'Alice, follow your mysterious heart.'

Pulled by the distant sound of quacking ducks, Alice and Bertie together climb the little track. Feeling uplifted despite the uneven stones under her feet, "How strange?" she reflects, "This is the track that we came up last night. I don't remember any ducks - only a beautiful cockerel shed."

This daylight colour is bright, tingling and intense; the sky a special kind of blue. The message - 'You are more incredible than you realise' - echoes with each and every step.

Walking hesitantly through the large wooden gate, she gasps in astonishment, "My goodness!"

19

A New Awareness

Still and quiet, a flowing land of gentle rolling green protects this carefree place of delicate, little creatures that have for some time lived almost undisturbed.

Discovering a precious sunlit jewel of many sights and sounds that lie within herself, she awakens with a sharp jolt.

Almost disbelieving, Alice declares to Bertie, "Why did I not see this before?"

Bewildered, she scratches her head. "What an amazing place! There is the cockerel shed - how did I not see any of these creatures before?"

"Here is a place I didn't imagine existed."

"This has a strange feeling of home," a puzzled Alice murmurs, "although I know that I never been here before!" She turns to see that Bertie is content and at ease amongst the unfolding of life.

Arising from beyond, a landscape of beautiful shapes, colours and sounds, a universe of delicate sensations now begin to flood her fragile mind, causing her body to shake.

In awe she exclaims, "The world looks bigger!", her lips quivering as she seeks to explain the uproar that she feels.

Surrounded by a place of so much colour, variety and life,

feelings that have no name are felt far deeper than the limits of her understanding.

Encountering unfamiliar thoughts and emotions, she cries out, "I cannot possibly have all of this within me - where do I start?"

A place that is imperfect with fear, anger and sorrow... and yet still so full of joy, hope and playfulness.

Quietly, gently, little chicks begin to gather by her feet.

20

Unsteady Steps

Spinning, swirling, a contradiction of emotions, wobbling on her feet, Alice takes a sharp intake of breath, as these little creatures gather around.

"How am I supposed to be in this strange place - a land of new sights and sounds?" Her voice breaks with the strain and panic of what she feels.

Confused, Alice yells, "One moment I feel anger and fear, and the next I feel confident and happy."

An excited Bertie scampers through her feet - caught up with the simple joy of being here.

"It's as if I can't trust myself," she howls. "I feel unable to let go."

Doubting her ability, she steadies herself as, fragile step by fragile step, she begins to relax into dancing with the colours of life as it is in this moment.

Passions bubbling - emerging into the empty space of life - she allows herself to feel ever more deeply amidst these new surroundings: this brave young woman.

Transforming fear and uncertainty, love and care arise and she begins to experience sudden, brief moments of joy and calm.

A single pivoting moment in space; although unsteady, with

courage she holds balance with the uncertainty of life - and witnesses her vulnerability without feeling afraid.

Continuing to trust, with gentle steps, she lets go... allowing more of herself to be known.

A soft, tentative smile settles across her face.

21

Quiet Tenderness

Reaching out from a safe yet lonely place, with a delicate, tentative touch towards these creatures fragile and small, feelings quickly arise for Alice within the commotion of this busy place.

Grappling with the constantly changing movement of life - quacking ducks, clucking hens and the shrill, elevated crowing of a splendid cockerel - she feels trapped. "It is as if my heart and mind struggle to be free," she sighs wistfully.

A deep breath reveals a greater truth beyond her thoughts. As each sensation ebbs and flows, this energetic, changing place now gives way to calm.

In a world that can be so difficult, she wonders, "Is this stillness real?"

A frown disturbs the soft features of her face. "I don't feel very strong."

A fluffy, radiant yellow chick, full of life and hopeful yet trembling, steps faltering towards Alice, eager to be known.

Pulled by her tender heart ever deeper into this passing, fragile moment of time, warmth and joy flow within her.

Bertie, now distracted, is immersed in curiosity as an enquiring chick looks on.

"So much of what concerns me takes place only in my mind," she ruefully reflects, with calmness settling in her voice.

A place of moments, where 'I' am only temporary - a growing, changing part of this wonderful, unfolding pattern of life.

Her many emotions, regardless of how much she fears them, are tender, precious gifts that guide her; a vivid rainbow of living sensations.

Just like these precious little creatures, they long to be seen, cared for and known - to be experienced and felt in each and every moment.

"By holding on too tightly... I see that I cause myself pain," she recognises, as she rises to her feet.

22

A Breathtaking View

Passing the cockerel shed, Alice and Bertie climb a narrow hedge-lined track that winds behind wide rolling hills, and shelters this place from the world. Turning a corner, she is greeted by a sight so extraordinary that it takes her breath away.

"Oh, my goodness!" she exclaims, standing still.

Stretching before her is a vast, incredible landscape of rolling green fields, coloured stone, purple heather-covered hills and steep, tumbling ridges.

"This is beautiful!" she utters breathlessly.

Gullies and tracks drop gently towards a patchwork of green, criss-crossed by weathered stone walls that dip and wriggle within an immense kaleidoscope of changing, flickering light.

"I feel so small," murmurs a pensive Alice. "This place is astonishing, and so much bigger than me."

She ponders, "These amazing sensations must have always been here... yet I feel as though I am experiencing them for the first time."

Above her, the gentle, warbling call of a curlew; below her, a field glows golden, honey-coloured yellow in the early afternoon sun.

Loving and caring, sheep lie exhausted in the long grass, as they watch their new-born wobble unsteadily to their feet.

Alice smiles in recognition, "It is not that the world has suddenly altered... it is that I am different."

Quivering with excitement, "A change is taking place in me!" she observes.

The tug of her heart ever stronger, she strides with strength and confidence through this brilliant land, declaring, "I feel so alive!"

23

Confidence Grows

Pulled by her deepening sense of joy, she reaches a small forest. "Look - another path for us to follow," says Alice curiously to an attentive Bertie.

Descending a small, steep dirt track that twists and turns its way downwards, towards the low-lying farmland of the dale, Alice and Bertie follow a sharp bend past a large wooden barn.

"Oh, my goodness - look at this, Bertie!"

Excitement quickly turns to shadows in her mind. "I'm not sure if I am meant to be here?" she sighs nervously.

"Perhaps I have taken a wrong turn?" - the echo of an anxious child stirring broodily in her voice.

With the trickle of a gentle stream, small birds singing and soft leaves rustling in the air, she takes a deep breath and feels peace and confidence once again.

Deciding not to allow these doubts to overshadow the beautiful, growing light within, "I... I'm going to carry on... and allow what I do not yet understand time to gently unfold."

Continuing down this path, through the shadows, Alice reaches a sign that reads, 'Dale Head Farm Tea Garden.'

"Ah! I have found something wonderful!"

With a growing sense of anticipation, she whispers, "I wonder what there is for me to discover here?"

And with this thought, Alice and Bertie walk on, gently warmed by a soft breeze.

24

This Beautiful Place

Past hawthorn and mayflower-scented blossom, Alice treads cautiously onto a large, weathered stone step and into a garden that is peaceful, still and calm.

Greeted by a warm, confident smile, she sits sheltered by a stone wall.

Delighted, her eyes catch every detail of this scene.

"What an amazing, restful garden!" Alice gasps, looking towards a contented Bertie.

Swallows dance in the air and a warm breeze blows across her delicate face as she sits, resting ever deeper into each and every sensation.

Sounds come and go as, moment by moment, past experiences now feel as though they have led her to this very place.

"There is so much to remember about my life," she murmurs, shifting restlessly in the chair.

"My loving Mum and Dad, caring Grandad and Grandma." A flood of thoughts fill her mind as she sits here, alone.

"Here you go, my dear," - this instant broken by a voice, gentle, warm and caring, as a delicious piece of cake and a pot of refreshing tea are placed beside her.

"This beautiful place," she sighs wistfully.

"My parents would be so happy to see me here." Her hopeful eyes fill with tears.

Passion coursing through her, "There is something precious that I hold within."

25

Awakening to New Sensations

A thoughtful voice enquires, "Have you enjoyed yourself?" Standing still, "Yes," replies Alice, a large smile quickly growing across her face.

Warmth brimming in her voice, "I have enjoyed myself a great deal."

"Well, if I can prepare the hot tub for you - please let me know." This invitation hangs in the air.

"For me?" a surprised Alice utters.

In this quiet moment, filled with a smile, Alice looks shyly towards the floor. "Well, I suppose, uhm, well... yes, I mean..." she mumbles, shifting awkwardly from side to side.

Gently, patiently, lifting her gaze upwards, "I think I will!" she encourages herself to reply.

Slipping into the gorgeous bubbling water, a chocolate box of melting caramel emotions begins to linger and tingle gently, far within the soft, aching muscles of her tired, precious body.

Swirls of steam all around, tiny bubbles dance intimately on the surface of the warm water.

Submerged, she now feels held and caressed, as if being cradled in her mother's warm, loving arms.

Resting completely, ever more deeply, instant by instant, she begins to awaken to the marvel of her being.

With a growing sense of self-love, she hears the earth softly whisper:

"Care for your dreams, dear Alice,
This world is yours for the asking,
Relax, and trust in the mystery within,
You are meant to be here, gentle child."

26

Deepening Experience

Relaxing with kindness into this beautiful garden, Alice watches intently and calmly as light glints and shines while shadows rise and fall.

"I cannot believe this is me - I have experienced sorrow and joy so deeply here... and yet I feel stronger!"

A trembling sensation ripples through each fibre of her body as she realises, "I hold within me a powerful universe of emotion." In that instant, Alice recognises that this is her gift.

Throwing herself into the air, arms outstretched, "I feel so alive!" she giggles breathlessly.

Awake to the uncontrollable brilliance of it all, insight - fragile and quiet - flickers, while emotions stir deeply in her passionate heart.

Allowing herself to feel more fully has released her from the well-worn habits of her mind, revealing a path to a new and deeper understanding.

For a moment, Alice is fearful of being hurt. "Soon I'll be going home, and leaving this place of safety, rest and care."

This inspires a thought: "It is impossible for me to escape all unhappiness. By accepting my feelings at these difficult times I can at least pause and consider the most helpful approach."

Standing still and calm, her voice hushes. "Could this be true for us all?"

Glancing towards the weathered stone wall surrounding the garden, she notices a young man walking slowly by. Arms wrapped tightly across his body, his eyes are downcast.

Kindness rises in her heart, "I wonder if he understands this too?" Her question lingers in the fresh breeze of this cloudless afternoon.

Alice turns to Bertie, and his crumpled brow relaxes with the warmth of her loving smile. "Even though I am unsettled by change, I can walk in this world, choosing to grow in love and compassion with each and every step that I take," she declares.

Emotions now far too complex for her to put into words, she winks, "Come on boy, there is so much to discover and explore."

With less hindering her, Alice walks through the gate and along the road that will eventually lead them both back home.

Epilogue

A clear blue sky above her and Bertie by her side, Alice peers down the heavy, empty tracks that curve and dissolve into the rolling landscape.

Memories of feeling anxious and alone at home collide with the stillness and calm of being here. "I am still nervous about going back," she realises. Her heart pounds with apprehension as the bulk of a large train approaches this remote country station. Minutes later, Alice and Bertie are aboard.

Stretching her legs under the table, with Bertie at her feet, a loud conversation intrudes upon the sense of quiet she feels within. Alice closes her eyes, concerned that these new gentle sensations might not survive the busyness of everyday life.

The view outside becomes a blur of green as they race through the countryside. Blue skies and sunshine eventually give way to a blanket of grey cloud, as the changing landscape gradually becomes more familiar. All too soon, Alice finds herself walking wearily into the street where she lives. Her body aches and her mind is swirling with stories of what she will encounter.

Her muscles relax as she cautiously opens the door, and is greeted by the faint yet familiar smell of her home. There is no sound... only an empty place of half-forgotten memories. Her heightened senses listen and look for any sign of change.

Stepping inside, this tired figure feels daunted, remembering the strain and uneasiness she felt before leaving.

Lovingly watching Bertie, with his eyes wide and tail wagging, find his blanket and settle down, Alice recognises her own need to rest. "I need to take care of myself," she murmurs, moving towards the kitchen.

Swirls of steam rise slowly from a cup of tea as she sits, gazing onto the busy street below. "How can I have experienced so much... and yet nothing here seems to have changed?"

Unsettled by a nagging doubt, "I don't want to lose the gentle kindness and patient understanding I have discovered - I care about who I am."

Sitting in quiet solitude, this sensitive soul puzzles, "Yet, before I left, I could not have imagined feeling like this!"

Cream cotton curtains soften the afternoon light and cause shadows cast by objects in this room to be barely visible.

Breathing slowly, Alice tiptoes through these precious moments in time where insights flourish. "My mind cannot be fully aware - or it would have known what was going to happen to me," she whispers.

Witnessing a deeper truth, her body trembles with excitement and anticipation. "The thoughts I have are not the reality of how this world really is."

"What do I do now?" she sighs.

With nowhere to go, Alice collapses back into the chair. Resting beside her, Bertie raises an eyebrow. Silence sucks the air from the room as, in this moment, she feels the weight of this new-found understanding.

"Life is about seeing and experiencing the world as it really is... not as I think it should be." Tears well in her eyes.

Taking a comforting sip of tea, this young woman realises that she is tired of being caught up in a continuous stream of ideas that run like a ribbon through her mind.

Perfectly still and breathing deeply, she sits not uttering a word as clarity takes hold. "Each moment brings with it the precious opportunity to believe and create a vision of how my life can be," she grasps.

Now more confident amongst the shifting light within this room, Alice rises and begins to once again immerse herself back into the flow of life.

At first, it seems as if there is little point to this quiet, elusive path. Her commitment to open to the landscape of emotions she experienced at The Tree unsettles and disturbs her.

But in time, loneliness and confusion ebb away as, like a vast, deep ocean stretching for miles towards an unknown inner horizon, knowledge of herself steadily grows.

Gradually, courageously, Alice learns to trust in the boundless possibilities of each moment, enabling her to face and steer her way through the changing, challenging realities of this world with greater ease.

· Parting Words ·

Have faith that there is a precious, incomprehensible gift that you hold inside. While it is fragile, hidden and quiet, its effect in your life can be powerful.

Be especially kind when you find yourself struggling, and know that Alice and Bertie will be with you, wherever you go.

The Tree The End

Follow Alice and Bertie at:

www.aliceandbertie.com